This is Charlie.

Sometimes she's cheeky.
Sometimes she's playful.
Sometimes she's full of mischief.
But always, her Mum and Dad think she's
the best little girl in the world.

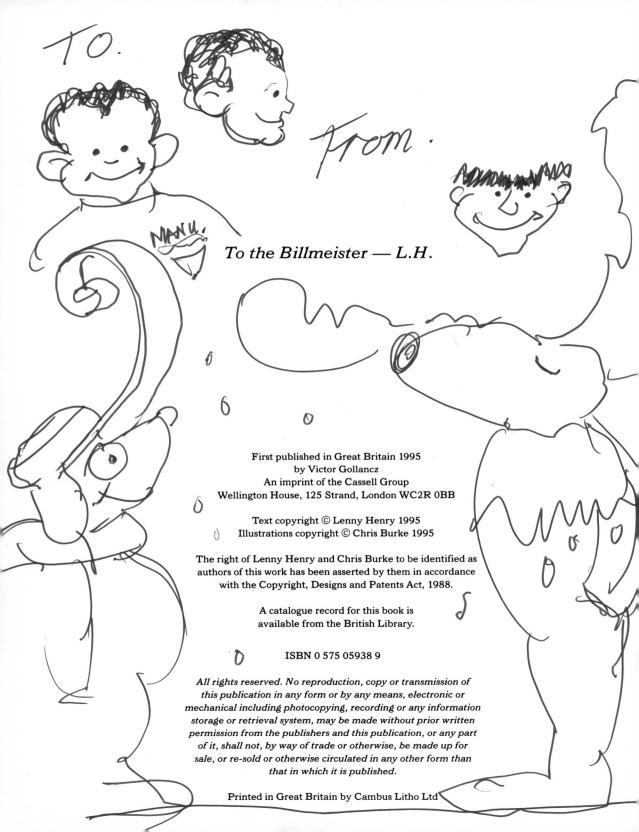

To the Billmeister — L.H.

First published in Great Britain 1995
by Victor Gollancz
An imprint of the Cassell Group
Wellington House, 125 Strand, London WC2R 0BB

Text copyright © Lenny Henry 1995
Illustrations copyright © Chris Burke 1995

The right of Lenny Henry and Chris Burke to be identified as
authors of this work has been asserted by them in accordance
with the Copyright, Designs and Patents Act, 1988.

A catalogue record for this book is
available from the British Library.

ISBN 0 575 05938 9

Printed in Great Britain by Cambus Litho Ltd

CHARLIE
AND THE
BIG CHILL

LENNY HENRY

Illustrations by
CHRIS BURKE

VICTOR GOLLANCZ

Charlie definitely, absolutely, positively
didn't like shopping.
Mum would never let her have any fun.

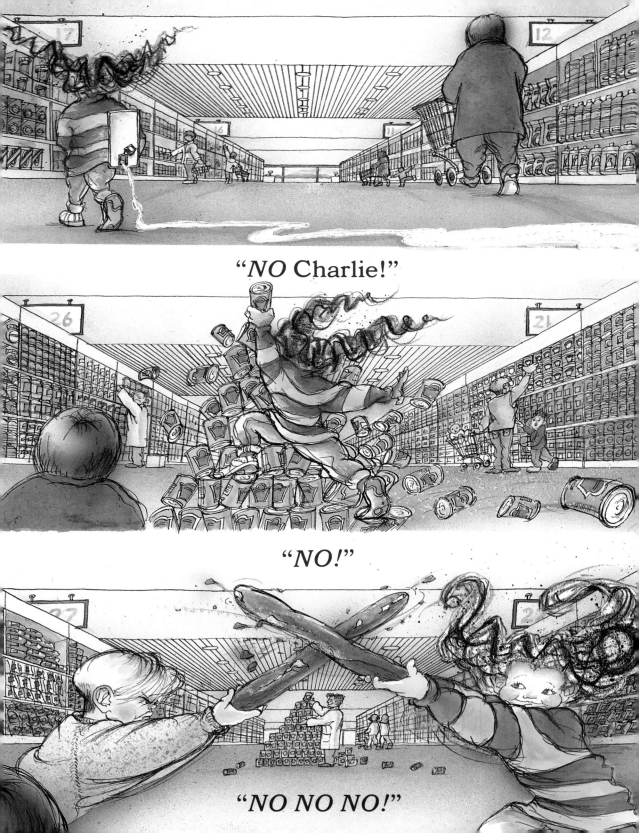

"Charlie, will you get me six large eggs, please?"

"Behave yourself — no touching the ice-creams!"

"If I can't stop at the ice-creams I'll just —

"Z I P P P P P P!"

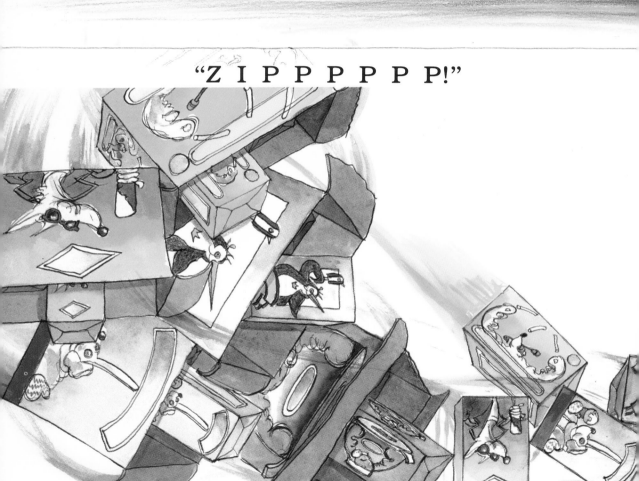

"O h h h h N O!"

— S L I D E   right past them."

"W o w e r o o n i e!"

"Who are you?"

"We're the Ice-cream Posse —

"Blinky, blonky, blimey — let's go!"

you're just in time for the disco."

Charlie taught the fox the 'Funky Chicken',

the bear the 'Boogaloo'

and the moose the 'Mashed Potato'.

Soon they were out of breath and
sat down to a frosty feast.

But Charlie wanted to explore
and set off towards the sun.

But it wasn't the sun at all.

It was an old, cold, gold egg.
Mum *would* be pleased.

Charlie was so excited,

she didn't notice her new friends disappearing.

It was the biggest snow giant she'd *ever* seen.

Actually, it was the *only* snow giant she'd ever seen.

As he chased her, he sang this song —

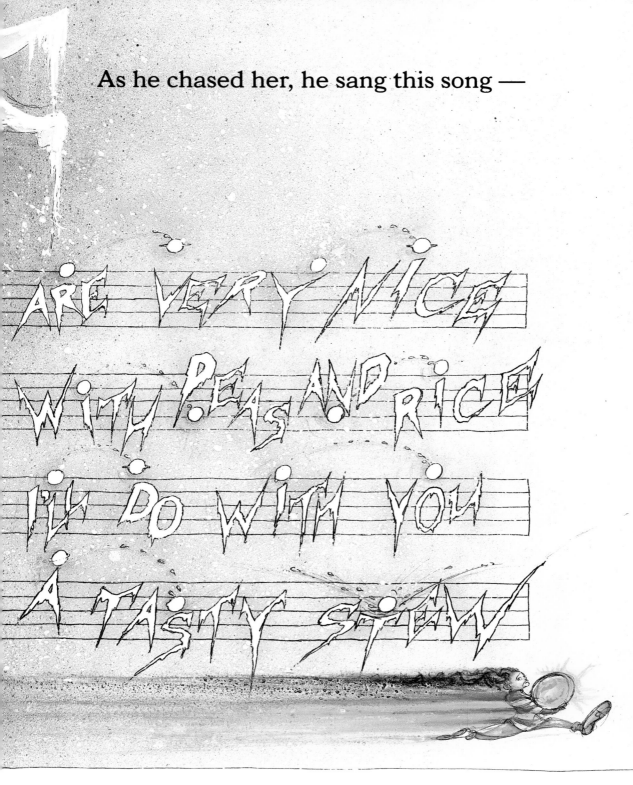

Charlie ran and ran and ran —

Bam palam — smack dab into Mum!
"Well done. What took you so long?"

Huh! Mums don't know anything about shopping.

The nice man helped load the car.

"Say thank you to the nice man, Charlie."

"Thank you."

"Phew!"

"That was brilliant!"